WHEELS AROUND

Shelley Rotner

Houghton Mifflin Company

BOSTON

For Stephen—What goes around comes around.

Special thanks to Hans Teensma.

Library of Congress Cataloging-in-Publication Data

Rotner, Shelley.
    Wheels Around / written and photo-illustrated by Shelley Rotner.
    p.   cm.
    ISBN 0-395-71815-5
    1. Wheels — Juvenile literature. [1. Wheels.] I. Title.
TJ181.5.R68 1995   94-35402
621.8'11 — dc20   CIP
                            AC

Book design by Hans Teensma/Impress, Inc.
Printed in Singapore
TWP 10 9 8 7 6 5 4

Wheels help
us to work and
play in many
different ways.

They help us get around.

Old cars, new cars, taxis, and limos.

Wheels take us places we need to go.

Buses carry us
around town
and to school.

Police cars
help keep our
neighborhoods
safe.

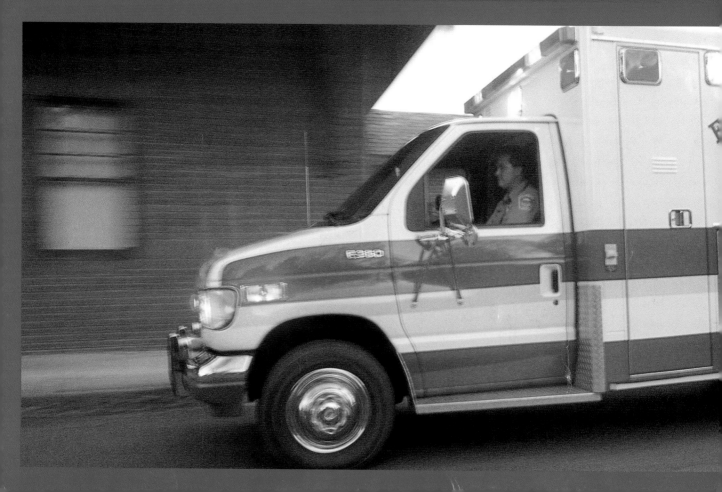

Ambulances
take sick people
to the hospital.

Fire trucks carry water, hoses,

and ladders to put out fires.

Garbage trucks take away our trash, mail trucks deliver letters, magazines and packages, and street cleaning trucks wash our streets.

Trucks deliver food to eat.

Tractors help farmers work the land.
Logging trucks move logs.
Horse trailers carry horses.

Wheels help move
heavy loads.

Tractor trailers
carry cars and tankers
deliver fuel.

Tow trucks pull cars and cars pull trailer homes. Moving trucks help us move our things.

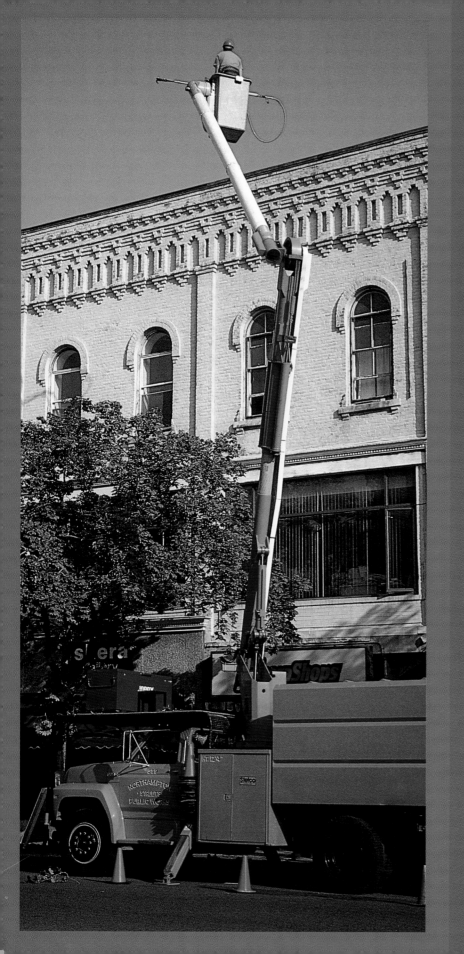

Wheels
help to fix and
build things.
Cherry pickers
lift, graders push,
and backhoes
dig and lift.

Cement trucks
mix and deliver
concrete.
Dump trucks
haul loads of
heavy rocks,
gravel, and dirt.

Wheels are always working for us.

Wheels Around.